AF375632

Claudia Haase

Christmas at Bergfels Palace

A lesbian romantic short story

Bibliografische Information der Deutschen Nationalbibliothek / Bibliographic Information of the German National Library:
Die Deutsche Nationalbibliothek verzeichnet diese Publikation in der Deutschen Nationalbibliografie; detaillierte bibliografische Daten sind im Internet über http://dnb.dnb.de abrufbar / The German National Library lists this publication in the Deutsche Nationalbibliografie; detailed bibliographic data are available on the internet at http://dnb.dnb.de

Edited by Sierra Campbell – Editing by Sierra

Printed and Published by BoD – Books on Demand, Norderstedt

Cover: Malkovstock, Calm image of interior Classic New Year Tree decorated in a room with a fireplace
Image file: iStock-628036942

ISBN: 978-3-7578-2943-8

Content

CHAPTER 1

Charlotte looked skeptically out of the train window. The train station in Bergfels was tiny. Would there be a restaurant in the station building where she could rest and eat after the long train ride? Or should she head straight to the hotel guesthouse first and unload her suitcase? There she could also have a bite to eat and then go on an exploratory tour of Bergfels.

The train came to a stop with a jolt. She shouldered her laptop bag and heaved the bulky suitcase out of the luggage net. A bag would have been more practical, but for the archive visit she needed finer clothes to appear more respectable to the Count.

Only a few people got off the train with her, and she was instantly alone on the small platform. There didn't seem to be a station restaurant, but a sign pointed to the pedestrianized center of town, where her hotel guesthouse was located.

A fine drizzle made her pull up her hood before walking purposefully in the direction indicated. It was hard to believe that in four weeks it was already Christmas. She had hoped for snow before she left for Bergfels. A photo of the palace amid a white winter wonderland would please her boss.

And my wallet. Otherwise, it would be tight with the dissertation. I'm afraid the Christmas presents for my parents will have to be smaller than usual this year.

There was not much activity on the main street, which was lined with half-timbered houses with small stores. Charlotte looked at the nicely decorated windows as she passed.

There was a wool store with handspun sweaters, scarves, and hats as well as a shop with pottery, woodcarvings, and paintings with palace motifs, followed by a small business with specialties from the region.

She was surprised to see no Christmas decorations anywhere. Not a fir tree or a light. Was there a reason for this?

She approached the marketplace in the center of town and enjoyed the view of the town hall, which had been built in a Baroque style at the beginning of the 18th century. All around, she spotted a butcher's store, a cobbler, and an insurance office, as well as a small café. The hotel guesthouse was on a street next to town hall, and she strolled, suitcase in tow, across the marketplace, where a few stalls were spread out. Busy farmers were packing their fruit boxes.

"Hey, you there!" one of the women called out to her. "Would you like to grab something before we pack everything up for the county food bank?" She pointed to a crate of red-cheeked apples.

Charlotte nodded and approached the market vendor. "I'd love to. I just got here and could use some fresh fruit."

The woman put two delicious-looking apples in a paper bag and added a banana and two clementines.

Charlotte dug out her purse, but the woman shook her head, laughing.

"No, no, it's free! A welcome from Bergfels Village. We sell here every day. You're welcome to come back another time for more fruit."

"I will for sure!" replied Charlotte, reaching for the filled paper bag.

"Do you have a place to stay yet?"

"Yes, I'm staying at the hotel next to town hall."

"That is a nice little guesthouse run by the Bader family. Good choice." The saleswoman nodded appreciatively. "I hope you enjoy your stay."

"Thank you, thank you very much," Charlotte replied and strode toward her accommodation in good cheer.

12

CHAPTER 2

Flordelis Mathilde Ida, Countess of Bergfels-Blumenheide, roared through the gates of the palace driveway in her Jaguar, the gravel flying off in all directions. As she drove by, she saw a frightened rabbit hop away and a small flock of sparrows flutter excitedly out of a bush.

With vigor, she rode three times around the small traffic circle in front of Bergfels Palace, where she used to have bicycle races with her brother as a child. She had to take advantage of the fact that no one else in the family was around and none of them could scold her.

She slowed down before she steered the luxury car serenely past the main wing and stopped in front of the garage entrance. She hopped out, stretched, and sucked in the fresh country air. She was too seldom here. She fished for her briefcase from the backseat. The practical, ancient bag had accompanied her to all corners of the world since her youth.

Hurriedly, she marched to the side wing, where the former servants' entrance was. The family preferred this entrance to the heavy door at the front of the main building.

"Countess, is there anything I can do for you?" asked Hanka, the family's long-time servant, after accepting Ida's coat. "Do you have any special requests during your stay?"

"Gee, Hanka, how many times have I told you to just call me Ida?"

"But the Count of Bergfels-Blumenheide specifically ordered me to call you that."

"Yes, but do you see him around here anywhere?" Ida made a sweeping gesture and turned once in a circle. Hanka frowned and stepped sheepishly from one foot to the other.

Ida sighed. Hanka was to be pitied. Was she even paid decently? Was there a minimum wage for servants? She had never given it a thought.

For her, it was inconceivable to have other people working in her city apartment. Even though she had grown up with domestic servants, she just couldn't get used to it.

"Would you like some tea and pastries, perhaps? Tonight, I can warm something up for you. The chef will not arrive from your parents' vacation home in the Alps until tomorrow."

I'm not hungry or thirsty, Ida wanted to hurl at the servant. Instead, she politely replied, "Tea and pastries will be fine with me."

Ida put on a friendly face and nodded to the woman. "Tonight, however, I am eating out in the village. You can call it a day after you serve me tea."

It wasn't Hanka's fault that her father had asked Ida to introduce the family archive to selected guests, mainly history researchers, and to answer questions.

As if old Georg, the equerry, couldn't do that. After all, he introduced me and my siblings to the family history in the horse stable and knows more than all of us together about this house and our ancestors. Georg's parents and grandparents had already been in the service of the Count's family.

But Ida had agreed to help in the archives on the condition that this year she would not have to celebrate Christmas with all her relatives in the palace. She was looking forward to a good book, a glass of wine in her apartment, and walks through the empty streets of the city center, while her fellow citizens were busy at home with eating Christmas geese or gift battles. Should she even treat herself to a small fir tree at Christmas?

She would use the days off to plan a spring bazaar for the children's aid organization she worked for. Few there knew her true identity. She preferred to stay in the background but knew how to exploit her contacts with financially well-off relatives and acquaintances for donations and potential grants.

A breeze brushed through her hair. She had almost forgotten how drafty it was in this large reception hall. There was modern heating and fireplaces only in the private rooms upstairs and in her father's office downstairs.

"Hanka, please bring the tea to my room after all."

"With pleasure, Count... Ida." Hanka did a curtsy and disappeared through a narrow passage into the kitchen.

Ida climbed the stairs to her private chambers and strolled past the portrait paintings of her ancestors without paying any further attention to them. In a few days, she would study their history enough to be fully prepared for the question-and-answer session with the guests.

There was a gap where a large painting had once hung showing her with her grandparents, parents, and siblings. After a sprawling argument among all the portrayed family members, her father had it moved in front of the archives.

She opened the door to her small suite and a pleasant warmth radiated toward her from the fireplace.

Good! Hanka had thought of everything! She decided to unpack her travel bag so she could soon drive to the village and pay a visit to her long-time friend, Melanie.

CHAPTER 3

Charlotte looked around enthusiastically in the hotel room that her employer had booked for her. Two watercolor paintings hung above the bed. One showed the village with its famous brook that marked the border to the neighboring community. The other picture showed Bergfels Palace. It was depicted a little too exaggeratedly for Charlotte's taste. The building seemed oversized, and there was also a brick tower that definitely did not belong to the palace and could only have come from the painter's imagination.

She quickly hung up her clothes in the closet and stowed her cosmetic bag in the bathroom. Thanks to the market woman, she didn't have to worry about a snack, so she decided to prepare for her visit to the palace archives, which was to take place in four days. She hoped that, in addition to the questions she had submitted in advance, she would be able to tease out some additional information from the Count.

She reminded herself to put her research for the dissertation on the back burner and to go through the questions for her article first. She had to draw the old gentleman out so that he would divulge a few juicy details and try to steer the conversation toward the rumors that were circulating in the tabloids: The Count's son, whose engagement to a princess filled the headlines, seemed to seek the proximity of an Italian pop singer quite often and had built himself a love nest in a villa in Tuscany. She already saw the headline in her mind:

"NEWS FROM BERGFELS PALACE:
COUNT OF BERGFELS-BLUMENHEIDE
IN PERSONAL CONVERSATION
WITH OUR AUTHOR CHARLOTTE WEINHOLD"

Her boss might not even include her name in the headline. He would probably put it under the article and delete it from the headline.

Of course, Charlotte was not so stupid as to believe that the Count would confess his son's love affair to a young female editor. But she was cheerful that she could at least elicit a brief personal statement from him if she played it smart.

What could go wrong? The ringing of her cell phone jolted her out of her thoughts.

It was surely her mother. Sighing, she accepted the call.

"Charlotte, you said you would call as soon as you arrived!" her mother's concerned voice rang out.

"Mom, I would have checked in later tonight. I just got into my hotel room. And I'm here in civilization, not in the middle of nowhere! Imagine, the hotel room is bigger and fancier than my one-bedroom apartment in the city. It's really too bad I'll only be spending a few days here."

Charlotte looked out the window and saw snowflakes floating through the air like feathers. *Maybe I'll get around to taking a picture of the snow-covered palace after all.*

"Yes, but still, it's a crazy idea to set out on such a long journey alone, just to spy on the Count."

Charlotte regretted that she had told her parents about her plans in the heat of the moment. The idea of meeting the Count in person and being allowed to visit the palace had enraptured her too much. Her mother's pessimism annoyed her. At the same time, Charlotte had been racking her brains for days to find out how she could elicit first-hand information from the Count.

"Mom, don't worry. Why did I attend various seminars on interview methods and learn personalized interviewing techniques during my studies? That has to pay off at some point. I'll get it done," she explained with optimism. "And if I'm quick and can take another photo with my cell phone showing the Count in a respectable pose in his palace, I'll have enough material in hand," she continued. She would add a few embellishments to the article. That should satisfy her boss.

"Let's talk on the phone again tomorrow. I want to rest a little now. I'll be in touch, okay?" That worked. Her mother sent a few more words of advice through the line before they ended the call.

She knew her mother only meant well and was worried. She had not even told her parents about the second task she had been given. This one gave her a serious tummy ache: she was supposed to find information about Flordelis Mathilde Ida Countess of Bergfels-Blumenheide.

Little was known about the second-born of the house and there were hardly any usable photos of her – except for older family photos that had been published in the press on ceremonial occasions. But where should she start her research?

The search engines always landed on the Count's family tree; there was no sign of a social media account. And if the Count was as close to his daughters as she was to her own father, it would be difficult to get any information out of him.

CHAPTER 4

The corners of Ida's mouth hurt from laughing so much and her cheeks glowed. The alcohol had gone to her head. But she just couldn't say no when her long-time classmate and best friend Melanie took a spin through her café and offered the last guests the homemade rum pot as a nightcap before heading home.

"That was really the last round now, otherwise we'll still be sitting here tomorrow morning." Melanie exhaustedly settled down next to Ida on the wooden bench. "While we're at it, I really need to go through my closet and look for something 'fancy.'" She drew quotation marks in the air with her fingers. "I did buy a costume three years ago for Klaus' parents' silver wedding, but I don't think it fits anymore. So, I guess I'll just have to get a new outfit."

"Do you have a party coming up?" asked Ida, but immediately regretted it. After all, it didn't always have to be a special occasion to buy something new to wear.

"No, Mom doesn't celebrate another milestone birthday until next year. But Susanne wants the annual sibling photo we give our parents for Christmas to be out of line. She wants us to come to the photoshoot dressed up. Klaus had defiantly said he'll go in jeans and a sweatshirt." Ida could vividly imagine Melanie's husband posing for the camera in old, worn-out clothes out of spite.

"And what do the others say?" she asked. After all, Melanie and Susanne had four other siblings.

"They think it's great. Of course, they have unlimited money and clothes." Melanie sighed loudly.

"Where am I supposed to buy something chic? Do you think I'll find something at Mrs. Seidel's store? Or at the costume shop in the neighboring town?"

Ida shook her head. "Definitely not."

At Mrs. Seidel's there was fashion for the more mature woman over 60, mainly knitwear in pastel colors. She eyed her friend and, in her mind, ran through her walk-in closet in the palace, where many fine pieces were waiting to be presented.

"You know what? I'll take a look at my place. I'm sure I'll have something suitable for you."

"But you're taller than me," Melanie interjected.

Ida waved it off. "If necessary, we'll cut back! When is the photoshoot?"

"Tomorrow." Melanie grimaced. "I'd totally forgotten; there was too much going on at our place. Susanne is in the neighboring town in the late afternoon anyway, so she booked an appointment at the photo studio there. She always chooses the most practical way and doesn't have to invest a lot of work, time, or money," Melanie complained.

"Then come with me straight home. We'll pick out a dress or costume for you, then there'll be plenty of time to shorten."

"Ida, *von und zu!* You don't seriously believe that Old Mrs. Schneider from our tailor shop will find time for me, the commoner, tomorrow morning. She will probably have to get the right sewing thread for your clothes first."

Ida waved it off. "I didn't think about Mrs. Schneider at all. Hanka can shorten it for you. She has often sewn or shortened our clothes."

"Really?" For a second, Melanie's eyes lit up, but quickly a haze settled over her face again. "I can't pay for that. Especially because of the loss I'll have if I have to close the café early tomorrow to get to the photo studio on time."

"You won't have to do either," Ida said. "I'll hold down the fort here. Your temp Tina can help me. Nothing will go wrong for a couple of hours."

Melanie looked a little skeptical.

"Don't you trust me? When you opened the café, I helped you out, remember?"

"That was more than fifteen years ago, and I didn't have these expensive barista machines in my café back then," Melanie muttered. In the end, however, she agreed. "Oh, what the heck! It'll work out."

"You won't regret it. I'll do my best," Ida promised. "Now make sure the last guests leave the café so we can find you something to wear!"

"But we'll take my car, since I've only served and not drank anything. I'm not scrambling up the mountain to your palace."

CHAPTER 5

"I forgot that our new cleaning lady starts today. She should be arriving any minute. Make sure she mops up the entryway and the tables in front of the fireplace so I can set everything up later for tomorrow's mourners. Wait a minute!" Melanie disappeared into the kitchen and returned a few seconds later with a small booklet. "It says where everything is on here, so she shouldn't have any trouble."

Melanie puffed out her cheeks and looked pretty beat up despite the light blush on her cheeks and the hint of eye shadow that high-lighted her blue eyes. "Tell her I'll be back in the afternoon around five at the latest so we can get to know each other better."

"You haven't seen her yet?"

"No, we just talked on the phone. She just moved to our town yesterday and heard about the vacancy here through Mrs. Mueller at the supermarket."

"Does the new cleaning lady have a name?"

"Oh, yes, of course. Maria. Maria Hofner." Melanie sighed. "I should have canceled the photoshoot." She furrowed her brow enough to make Ida worry about her eyebrow makeup.

"I'll work it out," Ida replied, annoyed. "If you dawdle any longer, you'll be late for the photoshoot. And don't rub your eyes or you'll smudge all the pretty makeup I put on."

"Yes, Mom."

"And one more thing..."

"Yes?"

"You look great! The dress suits you; you look like a rich noblewoman. Klaus will look twice when he sees you, I bet! And Linus will be looking for his mother, since he won't recognize you at all." With this statement, she put a smile on Melanie's face.

"Really?"

"Yes, I am completely serious." Ida nodded in affirmation of her words. "And dear Susanne's eyes will fall out with envy for once."

"Oh yes, please!"

What Ida didn't tell her friend was that she had secretly slipped Klaus a handsome suit from her brother. And for little Linus, she had picked out a smart *Janker*, a traditional Trachten Jacket from the chest of traditional costumes they had worn as children. Melanie would be amazed!

"I hope Klaus gets to daycare on time and doesn't stroll around with Linus on the way," Melanie said, worried now, as if she had guessed Ida's thoughts. "They still have to change."

Ida adjusted her flat cap, under which she had tucked her blond bun. A piece of straw trickled down. She quickly picked it up. During the joint cleanup with Georg, she had completely forgotten the time.

It was outrageous that her father had entrusted old Georg alone with the tasks in the stable wing, when the renovation work on the stables was to begin in just one week. Hanka, the good soul, had fortunately reminded her that Melanie was waiting for her, otherwise her friend would rightly be angry with her now.

In her jeans and old fleece sweater, she felt really shabby next to Melanie. But she didn't have time to change. She had hurriedly accepted the altered dress from Hanka and merely exchanged her riding boots for the clunky hiking boots she had found in the tack room.

"Tina will join you in an hour, so you won't be here alone," her friend explained, reaching for the silver clutch Ida had also lent her. "You can't fit much in one of those handbags." Ida held the door open for her friend, but Melanie still made no move to leave. "Totally impractical, if you ask me."

Only fleetingly did Ida's eyes fall on a young woman standing hesitantly in front of the café, while Melanie continued to lament, "Gee, the entrance looks all wet! And all those footprints... I'll have to be careful not to slip with those expensive shoes." Overdrawn, she tripped around on her tiptoes.

"Yes, Countess," Ida joked, indicating a slight bow. "By the time you get back, our new cleaning lady will have everything spick and span."

"Excuse me, I..." the young woman in front of the entrance coughed and pushed her pom pom beanie out of her forehead.

"Come on in, it's open," Melanie greeted, making a welcoming hand gesture.

Such a slender, graceful appearance, and a beautiful face to match, Ida thought. She took a step back to clear the way and then regarded the person with an intense gaze. *High cheekbones and doe-like eyes, wow!*

The young woman strode through the door that Ida was still holding open, turning to face Melanie as she walked and – *splat* – slipped on the wet floor.

Startled, Ida slapped her hand over her mouth, unable to do or say anything, while her friend was already leaning down and helpfully reaching under the young woman's arm.

"Jeez, did you hurt yourself?" Melanie asked with concern, but the young woman just grumbled to herself before venting her displeasure.

"This place really needs a wipe."

That seemed to have been the cue for Melanie.

"Oh, you're the cleaning lady? Glad to see you're on time. We were just talking about you."

"Uh, I..." The woman seemed to hesitate for a moment, as if she were reconsidering the job. "Yes, I am," she said, nodding her head vigorously. "Excuse my curiosity, Countess of Bergfels-Blumenheide?" she addressed Melanie directly, who blushed and giggled away like a young girl. "I am..."

But Ida interrupted her before Melanie could explain the situation. "Yes, Ida... I mean, the Countess is late, she has to go to her next appointment. The photographer is probably already waiting."

Puzzled, Melanie looked up at her, but Ida emphatically pushed her into the street and whispered in her ear, "And don't you come back to me before five, you hear?"

Without further ado, she decided not to clear up the misunderstanding. That way, she might have a chance to get to know the woman better – without scaring her off right away or being confronted with prejudices. She was completely unromantic and didn't believe in such things as love at first sight. But something fascinated her about this Maria. She felt as if she would miss something if she didn't make the acquaintance of this stranger who had sailed at Ida's feet with vim and vigor.

"But..." Melanie started, only for her friend beat her to it: "And I don't have time for you now either, Ida, you can see that our new cleaning lady has to be trained," she said in conclusion, feeling at that moment like the perfectly responsible café owner she looked like.

CHAPTER 6

What a stupid thing. She met the Countess of Bergfels-Blumenheide, the daughter of the family her boss wanted more information about, in person and couldn't get a word out. This beautifully dressed person must have been the second-born, Flordelis Mathilde Ida Countess of Bergfels-Blumenheide. There was a slight resemblance to the young girl in the old photos on the internet.

No doubt. Charlotte would have loved to touch the velvety, heavy fabric of the dress. Such a noble thing! At least she now had another job. In this way, she could test how it would feel if nothing came of the interview and her dissertation and she had to earn her living by cleaning.

No! It wouldn't come to that; she had switched gears in a flash. After all, this café owner with the funny cap and the straw residue in her hair seemed to be a friend of the Countess. At least they had called each other by their first names. Maybe she could get some background information that way?

"Maria Hofner, right? I'm Melanie, the café owner," her counterpart introduced herself with an engaging smile.

Charlotte nodded and sent up a prayer to heaven that the real Maria would not appear at that moment.

"Yes, exactly. You can call me Maria," she replied in a firm voice. "What do you want me to start with? Maybe mop the entrance first, before any other guests get hurt?"

If they dared go in at all, given the bedraggled look of the boss. Charlotte shook her head. *I should be happy. The more I have to do here and the longer I stay, the more opportunities I have to question this Melanie.*

After just one hour, Charlotte knew she would never make a good cleaner. Her arms ached from the heavy mop she used to mop the café floor. No sooner had she cleared the entrance area of the slush than new guests walked in. She could have freaked out! Thanks to the thaw outside, her mood had sunk to zero, and her photo of the snow-covered Bergfeld Palace became a distant memory.

In the meantime, Tina, the temp, had arrived and was ordered to the kitchen by her boss immediately after her arrival for whatever reason. Loud laughter came from over there to her. *Should I perhaps serve the guests on the side?*

"When you're done with that, why don't you wipe down the big empty table back there? After that, you can turn your attention to the toilets," Melanie's voice sounded.

Surrendered, Charlotte nodded and lifted the heavy bucket of water. Tomorrow, her muscles would be terribly sore. And her arms would be a few inches longer. She was already looking forward to the warm shower in her hotel room. At the height of the counter, Charlotte was intercepted by the temp.

"You haven't been doing any cleaning for a long time, have you?"

"Huh?"

"Is this the first time you've cleaned? You left out the corners. And look over there! There's a puddle left. But don't worry, I won't say anything. It's your first day here. Just a moment..."

She reached over the counter and grabbed a small booklet on which was written *PROTECTION CONCEPT WITH HYGIENE PLAN FOR THE CAFÉ PLUS RULES FOR OCCUPATIONAL SAFETY.*

"I'm sure this will help you. It pretty much says how to tidy up this place. You should learn it by heart. After that, you won't have any more problems and you'll know exactly what to do and where things are."

"That sounds good, I'll do it." *Geez! How am I supposed to do that and take care of the interview and the research for my dissertation at the same time?*

"Maria? Would you like to take a short break and have a coffee with us?"

Charlotte turned around to find this Maria person, but then she remembered that she had pretended to be Maria and the offer was meant for her.

"It's a little idle right now, so we can use that time to get to know each other," Melanie suggested.

"Yeah, I'd love to. I'll just put this away," she said with a nod toward the bucket, the handle seeming to dig into her hand.

She rinsed the bucket out in the small laundry room between the kitchen and the bathrooms. A whole armada of cleaning supplies stood on the shelves. Cleaning rags, various brushes, and sponges piled up next to them. But none of the cleaning products looked like they would be suitable for the tables.

She should look in the little booklet. Maybe there was an answer in there. But first she should have coffee with her boss.

CHAPTER 7

"Maria? Out for a walk, too?" Melanie's voice rang through the silence of the small park that lay directly behind the hotel. One of the side paths led straight up to Bergfels Palace, Charlotte had found out. A little exploration in the fresh air was just the thing to get rid of the smells of the cleaning products that seemed to cling to her. In the meantime, it had even started snowing again.

"Hmm, yeah." Charlotte nodded. "I want to clear my head a little from work."

"I suppose you want to go up the path to the palace?" her boss guessed correctly. "It really looks magnificent at dusk."

Could Charlotte tell her that she was headed there? Doubts about whether she could continue to keep up her lie gnawed at her. At some point, the right new cleaning lady would surely get in touch with her boss, or word would get around that Charlotte had taken up residence at the hotel guesthouse and taken her job away. Then, when she showed up at the palace for a tour of the archives and the Countess was there for whatever reason and recognized her, her charade would be exposed.

"Will you show me the way? I've already considered turning back for fear of getting lost. The little paths all look the same."

"Let's go this way. It is easier to walk and also a little lit." Melanie gestured with her head to a hidden path that, on closer inspection, was tarred.

Collect yourself for a few moments, then confess to her that you are not the cleaning lady, Charlotte thought.

They walked along a narrow path lined with bushes, which led steeply uphill and made a bend after a few meters. As they turned the corner, the palace suddenly loomed in full beauty before them. A blanket of snow lay over the building, which was discreetly illuminated by a few advantageously placed lights.

"Wow!" Charlotte was speechless. "Your girlfriend truly lives like a noble," she blurted out after a few moments of silence. "Melanie? Where..."

Her boss had pulled back a little and leaned against a signpost.

"Beautiful, isn't it? I like the view. When I'm stressed from a long day at work and need a break from the café, husband, and kid, I sneak up there and imagine what it's like inside right now. Soon the Christmas decorations will be up on the outside of the palace windows. It's always fun to watch Georg and the old Countess in action when dictating the temps where the ornaments should hang up."

"You must know her well, the Countess and her family?" Charlotte tried again to find out something about the friendship status of the two women.

"Yes, Ida and I have known each other since our kindergarten days," Melanie answered frankly and heaved a deep sigh. "Where have the years gone?"

So I was right! Actually, this would be the ideal chance to ask more questions, if only it weren't for Charlotte's conscience, which was gnawing at her more and more with every passing minute.

"You're late with the Christmas decorations here, aren't you? There's not a Santa Claus, Golden Angel, or Christmas tree with fairy lights to be seen in the whole place yet," Charlotte remarked, quickly changing the subject. She couldn't just ask her about the Countess so unscrupulously.

"In our village it is an unwritten law that everything is decorated festively and cheerfully only after the commemoration of the deceased on the Sunday of the Dead as all people living here are very religious."

"Oh, and everyone really sticks to that?" Charlotte marveled. "It must be great and romantic to spend Christmas at Bergfels Palace! I love Christmas! I can literally hear the warm fire crackling in the fireplace all the way over here."

Inwardly torn between her job and her moral compass, she cleared her throat. She shouldn't... But did she have any other choice if she wanted to keep her job at the newspaper?

"Surely you could ring Ida's doorbell if you felt like it?" *Does one knock on the palace door? What's the usual thing to do when visiting friends at a palace?* "And do you have to check in with her first every time?" Charlotte just couldn't contain her curiosity.

Melanie laughed a beautiful, infectious laugh. Although Charlotte didn't even know what was so funny, she had to laugh along. She felt incredibly comfortable in the presence of her boss, she just realized. *I'm just going to let a little bit of time pass, then I'll tell her.* "Or does she have a chambermaid or a servant who makes appointments with you?" Charlotte thought aloud.

"No, oh God." Melanie hiccupped from the combination of laughing and talking. "She doesn't, no!"

How cute!

"A chambermaid! That's good!" Again, a hiccup shook her body. "She… Ida doesn't have anything like that," she repeated. "She's down to earth. Too bad she's… at the photoshoot today." She took an audible deep breath and seemed to listen to her inner voice. A few moments later, she had calmed down and the hiccup was gone. "Is it gone? Finally. What was I going to say? Oh well, if she were home today, you could have seen for yourself." She winked at Charlotte. "Come on, let's get back. The snow is falling too hard for me. Look, our coats are already all snowed in."

She approached Charlotte and gingerly patted the white splendor from her shoulders. In doing so, she came quite close, and Charlotte involuntarily held her breath. *If I were a snow woman, I would be melting right now,* Charlotte thought.

"Are you okay?" Melanie had taken off a glove and touched her cheek. It felt good to feel the warm, velvety hand. Melanie's perfume smelled heavy and a little tart.

No cheap perfume smells like that, it occurred to her. Maybe she had received it as a gift from her friend, the Countess, and used it every day to have at least a touch of prosperity around her and forget the stressful everyday life. She could well put herself in Melanie's place and her heart warmed up. *No, I'm not here to fall in love!*

Unable to answer, she avoided Melanie's gaze.

She noticed that a few stalks of straw were still stuck in her hair. Her boss was truly quite unpretentious, as she also seemed to help out in a stable in addition to her work in the café.

"You must be freezing; your boots are soaking wet!" Melanie snapped her out of her thoughts.

Charlotte looked down at herself. Her shoes were indeed drenched, and her feet felt uncomfortably clammy, unlike the rest of her body.

"I guess you're right. I didn't even notice." She wanted to turn around, but Melanie still held her cheek and eyed her intently. Charlotte swallowed. The scenery behind the Countess' friend was cinematic. Yes, this was exactly how Charlotte imagined the first love scene in her debut historical novel, which she planned to write for the lesbian world after she finished her dissertation.

She took a deep breath and closed her eyes for a second. Velvety lips touched her mouth. Or was it just a breeze and the kiss sprang from her wild imagination? *It couldn't have been. Melanie is married to a man, she has a son and she's a café owner in a small village!* Charlotte scolded herself.

"You're really shivering. Come on, let's move before we get stuck here!" Melanie clasped her shoulders and made her way down to the center of town. "What street do you live on?"

"At the hotel." *Confess already!*

Melanie blinked in wonder. "But you just moved here. Why are you staying at the hotel?"

"I'm not... I'm not a cleaning lady," Charlotte confessed spontaneously. "And my name isn't Maria, either. I'm a Ph.D. candidate earning my living at a newspaper. I have an interview appointment at the Bergfels Palace, and I'm allowed to use the archives for my research." She stopped and held out her hand to Melanie. "My name is Charlotte. Charlotte Weinhold."

Melanie looked at her piercingly and kept her distance. Hastily, Charlotte continued, "I'm sorry. It was a mix-up. If I'm honest, I thought I might be able to get information about the Countess through you. When I arrived at the café and noticed that you were quite close and on a first-name basis, it got away from me."

Whew. It was out.

"I realize, of course, that nothing will come of the information now. It was a stupid idea, I know," she added and tried to look as concerned, but also as honest and trustworthy as possible. Still, there was no reaction from Melanie.

"My boss really wants an inside story from the palace, otherwise he'll fire me. Then I can forget about my dissertation. I'd have a lot of time to do it, but no money."

What am I talking about? Melanie won't care at all. I'm not her problem!

"Woah, what kind of a person are you?" her short-term boss let out.

"I know you're upset. I totally understand. I would be, too. Nevertheless, I got carried away a bit. I can only apologize for my behavior."

CHAPTER 8

Ida racked her brain. The name of this young woman meant nothing to her. In any case, she could not remember having read Charlotte's name in any of the tabloids that reported on the high nobility.

When asked, Charlotte told her which newspaper she worked for. At least the name meant something to her. A friend of hers, Theodora, had worked there for some time before taking a job with the competition as deputy editor-in-chief. The insights Theodora had given her then into the work of the gossip newspaper were priceless.

Since then, Ida flipped through those magazines regularly. *Know your enemies.* In them, the same shrewd media representatives always reported on the noble families. And this Charlotte, of all people, was supposed to write a lurid article about her family? *I wonder if she had only recently started working there.* Anger crept up in Ida.

"You don't even realize that you're just being exploited by the newspaper, do you? You're promised God knows what and if you don't deliver, you'll end up on the street one day," Ida vented her indignation. "Every lurid word is published by these tabloids, but don't think they will just think of naming the real author." She almost added to her tirade how well she knew the tabloids and their makers. She had to control herself.

Why was she so upset? After all, she couldn't care less that Ma... Charlotte was allowing herself to be exploited and thus become a plaything of the glossy press.

For some inexplicable reason, however, Ida was concerned about Charlotte's – the name suited her much better than Maria – further path in life. This distracted Ida from the fawn eyes of the young woman, whom she had just breathed a kiss on the lips in a mad rush of romance.

Me and romantic all at once? It must have been Charlotte's fireside crush, that attracted her and led her to approach the young woman in this way.

She had better think about a solution as soon as possible, how she could straighten out her own tall tale. Sooner or later, she would be exposed. For a moment, she thought about putting Melanie in charge of the guests who had signed up for the archive tour, which obviously included Charlotte. But she quickly dismissed that possibility. She would only get entangled.

The family history of the Counts of Bergfels-Blumenheide was simply too convoluted and complex. Melanie could not possibly learn it by heart in a few hours, even if she already knew a lot from Ida's stories and anecdotes and was often a guest at the palace. That would stand out.

"I just don't want to squat in a part-time position where the profs pack me full of work that I couldn't even do full time," Charlotte defended herself. "And then research on the side!"

"And you don't care what the paper is doing? Now you're here, for example, and you're supposed to do an interview for an inside story. But I bet you were already aware on the ride over here that you're unlikely to get the internals your boss wants," Ida reflected. "That you're going to meet someone you can exploit; you couldn't have known then. How did you imagine that?"

"I won't take advantage of you and your friendship with the Countess. I just promised," Charlotte objected.

"But let's say you could do your boss' job. That's a lot of work. You have to prepare extensively, it takes time. You'll get a decent pay for it, I hope."

Charlotte turned pale.

"Now don't tell me you're doing all this for free?"

"No, the hotel room is paid for by the newspaper."

"What about travel expenses?" Ida asked. "And what about expenditures? Have your working hours been recorded so that you have enough time to take care of your dissertation? Otherwise, I don't see any profit in this employment. Especially since it lacks the scientific exchange you would have with your colleagues at the university."

Ida was at a loss. She didn't understand why Charlotte would do this with no pay.

"As a research assistant, you would have easy access to conferences and meetings, and you could apply for grants or small third-party funding, so that you could continue to research your topics after your doctorate. At the very least, the reputation of your dissertation supervisors could be of use to you sooner or later. The *Academic Fixed-Term Contract Act* shouldn't be a problem for you yet."

Charlotte swallowed audibly. "Don't be mad at me, but for a simple café owner, you've got quite an insight, I'll give you that. You sound like a university advertising brochure."

Ida swept the comment aside with a wave of her hand. "I'm just a bit older and rich in life experience. Many of my friends have studied or are even still employed at a university. That's where I get a lot of information."

"Gosh, sometimes I wish I had parents as rich as the Countess that lived in such a big palace!" Charlotte blurted out. "Not having to worry about anything, wearing fancy clothes, attending only the best schools and universities..." She slapped her hand over her mouth. "You probably hear the opposite from your friend all the time."

"What do you mean? Oh, sure, you mean Ida would probably prefer to live in a little hovel, completely unknown, or go shopping in jeans and a T-shirt at the farmer's market, with no paparazzi lurking behind the next bush? Sure, otherwise she wouldn't hide like that either."

"I think it's funny. I couldn't find her on any social media channel. Not even the official palace pages are reporting about her." Charlotte shook her head. "And in these times."

"True. She really does live a very secluded life," Ida agreed with her.

"Will you tell her who I really am and why I pretended to be Maria?" Charlotte hesitantly asked.

"No. You can tell her all about it yourself if you should run into each other in the archives. If you keep your promise and don't write a lurid article about Ida or the Count's family, I'd let the whole thing drop."

"That will not be the case. The Count will do the archival tour. That's what the invitation letter says." Ida could hear the relief in Charlotte's voice, who had no way of knowing that Ida's father would not be there.

"Possibly," Ida dismissed the misinformation for the moment. "Watch out, Charlotte. But tomorrow I will definitely need a cleaning lady. If the real Maria hasn't shown up by then, you can make yourself useful again," Ida said. "Paid, of course." She took it upon herself to take the wages out of the Count's private purse so that Melanie would not have any additional expenses.

***

Despite the late hour, Ida didn't miss the chance to drop by Melanie's place. She was too curious to see how the photoshoot had gone. After Melanie had reported in detail about her afternoon and raved about her two men in suits, Ida couldn't hold on any longer and unmasked Maria's true identity.

"Well, you two had the same idea and played nice." Her friend shook her head reprovingly. "When do you intend to tell her that you are the real Countess?"

"The right time hasn't come up yet. I'll think of something," Ida replied snappishly.

Did Melanie really need to remind her of that now? Still completely intoxicated by the events of the day, the words just tumbled out of Ida's mouth.

"I felt like I used to in school when we would jokingly switch roles. That was fun. Mari... I mean, Charlotte seemed to have no doubts that I was the café owner. Too bad she's only coming back to clean tomorrow. You really don't want to hire her permanently?" Ida asked, laughing. "But honestly, I don't know how long I could keep it up and serve the guests. Such stress!"

"You're lucky Tina played along!"

"I know. She acted like I was really her boss. And the only guests were a couple of women from the church choir."

"They must have looked perplexed that you work here!"

"Oh, come on, I let them in on it just in case. They really enjoyed the game, too, and clearly had fun driving me to the brink of despair with coffee and cake orders. Well, maybe my offer to pay for coffee and cake for the ladies contributed to that," she added with a twinkle in her eye.

Ida paused for a moment, feeling as if she were reliving the afternoon. "Poor Tina, she kept having to help me with the milk frother! I could hardly keep up!"

She studiously concealed the fact that she had spent much of the time surreptitiously watching Charlotte, who she found had performed her tasks with incredible ease and elegance, despite the now known fact that she was not, in truth, a skilled cleaner. "The rest of the guests were all tourists. When Charlotte comes to clean tomorrow, be sure to put on some fine clothes of mine again and play my part so she won't suspect anything. It was so nice with her… we got to chatting several times. Not to mention our conversation tonight."

"Chatting? She's supposed to be working, not chatting. You like her, huh?"

"What are you looking at me like that for?"

"She's pretty," Melanie noted, eyeing Ida closely, hands on hips.

Ida almost ranted, "Just pretty? She is a beauty and also very educated!" But she managed to bite her lips in time.

"What am I talking about? She's young, smart, and happens to be very pretty. And an aspiring doctor of history." Melanie seemed to have guessed her thoughts. "Whatever. I don't begrudge you the fun," she followed up.

"Wonderful! You know, she loves Christmas and wanted to know if I – that is, you – could just knock on my door at the palace," Ida recalled with a laugh. "I would have been too happy to invite her to my premises."

"Spare me further exposition of your gush!" Melanie interrupted her, stifling a yawn. "It's getting late, and I suspect the day has been exhausting for both of us. Will you pick me out one of your fabulous wild silk costumes? Something in dark green?"

"I'll see what I can do."

"Otherwise, I'm afraid our working relationship is over, and I won't let you work in my café anymore," Melanie goofed off.

CHAPTER 9

The next day, Melanie sat at a window table in the café in a dark green wild silk costume and made Ida slave away quite a bit. She clearly enjoyed placing each order one at a time and taking a lazy look out the window or keeping an eye out for the cleaning lady.

Just you wait, Melanie, Ida thought. *On my next visit without a disguise, I'll return the favor and let you serve me from front to back, too!* The knitting circle, which consisted of five older widowed villagers, knew the score, and Tina kept an eye out for other locals who arrived to let them in on it as well.

Ida was excited. More so than the last time. She hadn't been able to sleep at all, had only ever dozed off briefly and then dreamed of sprayed milk foam, which had inexplicably landed in Charlotte's pretty cleavage every time. *She's guaranteed not to come to clean up with her blouse wide open,* Ida scolded herself. There!

The door opened.

CHAPTER 10

Charlotte stormed into the café and threw Melanie a quick "Hello" and an apology for being late. She placed the bag filled with apples and clementines, which she had bought on the way from the nice market vendor, on the table. Breakfast would have to wait a bit. She ran straight into the small room to fetch the bucket and mop the floor.

Last evening, she had come across gaps in the Count's family tree and had tried during the night to close them with Google's help. In vain. One more thing she had to follow up on in the archives and that lengthened her list of bullet points. She had promptly overslept this morning, not hearing the alarm clock at first.

Only when she mopped the floor did she see the Countess in a dark green dress sitting at the table. Should she greet her spontaneously? *Countess, there are gaps in your family tree.*

But there was no opportunity to talk to the woman – the gardener of the Count's estate had to show up in the café with his hunting dog! With a loud call, he was ordered by the Countess to her table, startling the animal and causing it to race through the café with soaking wet paws.

It created a hopeless mess, knocked over Charlotte's bucket and swept over tables and chairs in fright. *Aren't hunting dogs supposed to be fearless?*

By the time Charlotte had finished mopping up, cleaning the tables and chairs, and tidying up the restroom, she noticed that the Countess had already made her way home. *What a bummer!*

Her back hurt and she had to prepare for the archive visit. Every day, the head of the editorial department bombarded her with tons of e-mails and suggestions on how she could get information.

Frustrated, Charlotte left the café in the late afternoon.

CHAPTER 11

A little nervously, Ida eyed the arriving crowd of guests, who gathered with cameras and bags in the small hall in front of the family archive. An older gentleman, the first to arrive, had already introduced himself with his business card as a university professor emeritus and asked to be given a separate interview appointment with Ida's father for his new book.

A little later, a young woman had appeared, a local reporter from the neighboring town. Three doctoral students from a renowned English university, who were beneficiaries of a grant from the Count's foundation, stood shyly a little apart.

A woman and two men from the Archive Association chatted quietly. Ida squinted at the list of people she held in her hand. The only one missing was a doctoral student named Charlotte Weinhold, whom her father had described as particularly well-informed and thirsty for knowledge. "She is writing her doctoral thesis on our family and is concentrating on our Portuguese relatives," he had told Ida that morning through his private secretary. He had been busy and had not been able to phone her, since he always devoted his mornings to the extensive study of the most important national and international daily newspapers.

Discomfort spread through Ida. She should have taken the chance yesterday to confess to Charlotte that she was not the café owner. Hopefully, she would take the game of hide-and-seek with humor.

Footsteps approached. Hanka was in front, and Ida could make out Charlotte's figure behind her. "Countess, now all the guests are complete. Our last invited guest, Ms..."

"Weinhold, I know," she quickly interrupted Hanka, who moved aside to reveal a perplexed Charlotte.

"Melanie?" she stammered, but rapidly seemed to put one and one together. "You're not Melanie at all. You're Ida," she stated.

Hanka shook her head indignantly and interjected in a loud and serious voice, "You must not talk to the Countess like that! To you she is still the Countess of Bergfels-Blu..."

"No, of course she can call me Ida," Ida interrupted the servant again and grinned at

Charlotte. The latter, meanwhile, did not seem at all pleased to see her. Rather, she looked as if she would like to turn on her heel.

Ida realized that her plan was not working, and that Charlotte obviously did not see the hide-and-seek game as a fun interlude. Now she had to see to it that it did not come to an éclat in front of the other guests.

She cleared her throat and threw a professional smile. Later, they could talk it out.

"Dear guests, I am pleased to welcome you here at Bergfels Palace on behalf of my father, the Count of Bergfels-Blumenheide," she started. "My name is Flordelis Mathilde Ida, Countess of Bergfels-Blumenheide. I am the eldest daughter of the family and will honor you today in place of the Count. You are fortunate to be among the selected few who have been granted permission to visit our family archives. I assume that you all already have a wide and profound knowledge of my family, in one area or another, perhaps even superior to me with your expertise..."

She paused, giving those present time to feel flattered. "Nevertheless, I will briefly give you an insight into the family tree of the Counts of

Bergfels-Blumenheide before presenting you with some precious items from our collection that might interest you."

The group nodded with satisfaction. Only Charlotte stood there with a petrified expression. At the sight of her, Ida lost her train of thought for a moment and had to force herself to fulfill her expected duties as host and not drag Charlotte into the library to explain herself.

"Afterward, you will have the opportunity to ask questions and – as approved by us – examine the archival documents you wish to see. We further on allow you two hours for inspection, but, of course, you already know that from correspondence with Dr. Buechlin, the assistant to our palace administration, who also sent you the rules of conduct for visiting our house."

Ida fed the guests information about the family tree of the Count's family, which reached back to the 14th century, and dropped in a few anecdotes here and there that Dr. Buechlin had gathered. Shortly before the end of her remarks, she approached a large painting that hung directly next to the entrance to the archive and showed all family members in extremely advantageous poses.

Enthroned above the family on the wall were the antlers of a 22-ended deer, which Ida's great-grandfather had supposedly shot during the last drive hunt conducted by Kaiser Wilhelm II. The difference in size between her diminutive grandmother and her hulking grandfather, who sat to the left and right of her sisters, was cleverly concealed by their seating positions.

Her youngest sister's expansive bosom and her middle sister's gaunt shoulders were hidden by immense, cleverly draped masses of fabric. Her father's arm, paralyzed by a stroke, hid behind her mother, who stood diagonally in front of him in elegant, velvety robes and with a truly aristocratic expression. Her brother stood between her father and grandfather, all three in smart uniforms and wearing numerous medals, and Ida filled the gap between her mother and grandmother.

Grandmama wore the traditional costume of the village of Bergfels to showcase her long-standing ties to the community. A heavy chain with a bulky cross was meant to emphasize her faith in God. Ida herself wore a slim silk dress embroidered with fine brocade threads. Palace dog Casimir lay at her feet, one front paw laid over the other, chewing contentedly on a bone. The artist had conjured an engaging smile on the lips of the assembled family members. Such a false ideal world!

My brother has a mistress in Italy, I'm a lesbian, and my youngest sister raps songs in disguise under an alias on stages around the world. And if that's not enough, the other one is planning to open a tattoo studio but has gambled away her entire inheritance and evaded taxes, so she has to keep her feet still for now.

All this posing and faking false facts! At least she had a clear conscience herself and had nothing to reproach herself for so far. She ignored the fact that she had recently played a false game and hurt a woman with it.

CHAPTER 12

Rain slapped against the windows of the newspaper's office and did nothing to lift Charlotte's spirits. She had arrived home late after her hasty departure from Bergfels, but even though she was quite worn out by the events, she had not been able to sleep through the night. That won't be helpful when a telling off from her boss was waiting for her that morning. She had completely missed her goal for the trip.

"If you don't present me with an in-depth interview with the Count of Bergfels-Blumenheide or an unbeatable inside story in the Christmas issue, you're fired!"

Anxiously, Charlotte ducked her head.

"I told you he wasn't on the scene and the Countess wasn't very communicative," she tried to justify herself. "I tried everything humanly possible to get info. That's all I could do."

"You can tell someone else, not me. Here!" Her boss threw a newspaper with the job ads open on the table.

"Did you know that the Count of Bergfels-Blumenheide is looking for a historian to spruce up the archives? I'll give you one last chance. Otherwise, I really don't know why I should still employ you here. After all, we're not a welfare office. You'll get the job and deliver something sensible. It won't be that hard to ask the staff there a few questions and snoop around a bit. You've been there before."

"What?" Charlotte nearly toppled from her chair. "But…"

Her boss raised his hand. "No buts and no excuses. You heard me." And he was out the door in a flash.

***

A day later, Charlotte's small apartment was dust-free, the curtains and drapes washed, the kitchenette sparkled, and the laundry was clean and ironed and tucked away in the closet.

For almost all of Saturday, Charlotte had been fussing around the apartment. All this time she had been fighting an inner battle over whether or not to call Melanie. It would be seven o'clock in a minute. Melanie was a busy woman and had enough on her plate with the café and her family.

Phone calls to a student whose future was unsure and who was consumed with lovesickness for a Countess were certainly not one of Melanie's favorite after-work activities. Why wasn't Ida, Melanie and vice versa?

Sighing, she dialed Melanie's phone number, which she knew by heart by now. When she had left the hotel in Bergfels with flags flying, she had run into the café owner on the way to the train station, who had pressed a piece of paper into her hand.

Carelessly, Charlotte had stuffed the leaflet with Melanie's phone number into the last corner of her jacket pocket. She hadn't felt like discussing anything with the fake Countess. What was she supposed to talk to her about?

On the way home, however, she had regretted her abrupt departure. Still, she had lacked the courage to contact Melanie until now.

It rang for a while until the café owner's rushed voice could be heard on the phone.

"Yes, hello?"

"Hi, Melanie." What a greeting. She should have thought about what she was going to say while cleaning her apartment. "It's Charlotte."

"Oh, Charlotte, you! I was beginning to think you'd never call and had disposed of my phone number. One moment, please!" Charlotte heard voices in the background, and it took what felt like an eternity before she came back on the line.

"Sorry, it's chaos here. The real Maria still hasn't shown up and because of cleaning at the café I'm always home late. Don't you want to keep working for me?" Melanie paused for a moment before continuing, "Just kidding. You're completely overqualified, of course."

"It was still fun," Charlotte replied. "Even if I was pretty knocked out afterward."

"By the way, I'm also sorry for pretending to be a Countess. Ida took such childish delight in it that I didn't want to keep her from role-playing," Melanie apologized in a rueful tone. "But you were so quick to run away that I didn't even get a chance to speak."

"Melanie, I... I don't know why I left without talking to you. I just wanted to leave and was frustrated because I couldn't concentrate on the files in the archive at all. During the Q&A session that followed, I couldn't get my mouth open. I couldn't direct a single one of my questions to Ida."

"And how can I help you? Should I ask Ida if she'll let you look at the archives?"

"No, I... Oh, Melanie. I don't know either. I can't stop thinking about her. But it hurts so much, she was just kidding around and leading me on. She can take her apology and shove it," the words tumbled out of her.

"Oh, she apologized to you already? She didn't tell me that."

"Well, she called the newspaper office a couple of times and wanted to talk to me. But I denied it."

"Well, well." Melanie clicked her tongue.

"It's... My boss wants me to apply for the vacant position at the palace archives so that I can get some inside knowledge. In the process, they're looking for someone reputable to work on the family history. But my boss sees it as a huge opportunity to snoop around there. If I don't do it, he fires me. No job, no money… well, maybe I should actually look for a cleaning job."

Charlotte could not hide her disappointment, as her future depended on this position.

"So, are you doing it?"

"Is she there?"

"What?"

"I mean, is Ida there? Not at the café, but at the palace? The interview is the day after tomorrow."

"No. She left abruptly after the tour and your meeting in the palace archives. Supposedly problems because of the Christmas bazaar, which she could only settle from the agency. You better believe it." Melanie puffed into the phone. "I'm sure she won't be showing up here again anytime soon."

"Well, if Ida were there, I would definitely not go to the interview. According to the advertisement, Dr. Buechlin, who handled the organization of the archive visit at the time, is supposed to be responsible for filling the position, so this information seems to be correct."

"And you really want to write a lurid story?"

"What choice do I have?"

"You do realize that after this you can't show your face here anymore and you'll be rid of the job in the archives? Ida is my best friend, and I can't stand it when she gets hurt. You won't have me to cry with anymore."

Charlotte nodded.

"Are you still there?"

"Yes. Of course, I'm aware of that. But what else would I do with the job in the archives? It is an excellent excuse to gain access for me. Don't be angry with me, but Bergfels is a village in the middle of nowhere. I'd be stuck there." She had only called Melanie anyway to find out if Ida was still present in the palace.

"Think it over! That's all I'm going to say about it."

CHAPTER 13

Ida pressed her ear to the heavy wooden door, which was slightly ajar, and listened intently to the recruitment interview that her father and Dr. Buechlin were conducting with Charlotte in the large reception room. For her part, it had not taken much convincing for her father to hire a historian for the archives. It had been more difficult to persuade her friend Theodora to let the job ad show up on the desk of Charlotte's boss through her old contacts.

Ida could have danced a polonaise through the palace in childish joy when Charlotte's name caught her eye while she was reviewing the applications.

"Ms. Weinhold, I am very impressed by your dissertation topic. So far, neither my parents nor my wife and I have paid any attention to the complex relationships of the Portuguese branch of our family," Ida's father elaborated. "In that respect, you would be the perfect person for the job. Of course, as part of the family chronicle, you will also have to illuminate the terrible sides of the war. Not to mention the noble connections to Salazar, which need clarification, as you rightly indicate in your exposé. We are well aware that our ancestors did not always act appropriately in those difficult times."

This was the difficulty of historical reappraisal. Ida knew that even though Portugal, as a neutral country, had not participated in World War II, there had been banks involved in the Nazi looted gold trade at the time. And some members of the family had maintained close ties with those same banks.

"You get the job," the Count of Bergfels-Blumenheide said in a patronizing voice. Ida could not breathe. Was he keeping the bargain she had made with him? For a few seconds, there was dead silence. Ida would love to see Charlotte's expression. Would she be pleased, or would she plan a revenge campaign to get back at Ida?

"On one condition, though," it resounded full-throated through the high-ceilinged room. "I have read some of your newspaper articles which you added to your application. I like your writing style. You will resign your position there immediately and spend the 23rd of December in our palace writing a benevolent exclusive story about our family. The goal is to finally and forever put an end to all gossip about our house and family." He cleared his throat. "My son and I will answer any questions you may have, and in closing, some of our family will be available for photographs. Unfortunately, my daughters will not be present at that time," Ida heard his sad-sounding voice. He paused for a moment and Ida heard him take a drink.

"The whole thing will appear in a special edition of the magazine *Interior Views from Noble Palaces,* in which we own shares, and which has an excellent reputation even in royal circles."

Ida could have jumped up in the air and clapped her hands loudly. *Dad, thank you!* Her father had done a great job and presented the condition in such a way that Charlotte had to agree. He should have become an actor.

His remarks suggested that she, Ida, would not be in the house. Her plans, of course, were different. She would give Charlotte the interview and ask her forgiveness again on that occasion. She also accepted the fact that she would have to spend the rest of Christmas with her family in the palace. Charlotte was worth it to her!

CHAPTER 14

"Then have fun with the young lady. I don't begrudge you that, seriously. I never thought you'd fall in love so tempestuously. Dad and I won't be back until ten o'clock at night. You know, there's a lot to organize for tomorrow's Christmas hunting before Christmas Mass." Ida's brother blew her a kiss and, laughing loudly, left their private quarters.

Under normal circumstances, Ida would have been insanely upset that her brother was making fun of her. *But what were normal circumstances now?* She had suddenly gone into a real frenzy after Charlotte had accepted the job.

Ida, together with Georg and Hanka, had set up a Christmas tree with numerous velvet-red bows and golden baubles in her private living room in the palace. Candles, some of which she had also distributed around the room, provided a sparkling play of light. All the Christmas cards that she had received from her extensive family and friends, which she usually let disappear directly into the wastepaper basket, stood this year on one of the two mantelpieces, under which the fire crackled.

A four-story Christmas pyramid perched as an eye-catcher on her great-grandmother's old ornate wedding trunk, and the rising air from the candles burning on the outside of the pyramid, spun the impeller clockwise. Crocheted, embroidered or bobbin lace tablecloths lay on the tables.

An elaborately painted tea service and two small bowls of homemade vanilla crescent cookies and walnut cookies, which her friend Theodora had slipped to her before she left for Bergfeld Palace, stood ready. Steaming in the pot was a high grade Chinese Qimen black tea from Anhui province, the best she had been able to find, with a light fruity aroma and a hint of pine.

Pine nuts! She had wanted to collect them in the forest and put them on the mantelpiece. *Too late!* The playlist, consisting of loud maudlin Christmas songs, was waiting to be started through her smartphone.

All in all, her living room exuded a homey atmosphere in her eyes. It was just right for the upcoming debate and interview.

Ida looked at the large grandfather clock, which showed just before five o'clock. She had to get changed because Charlotte would be arriving soon. She had decided on a casual look that was not too pretentious, but also not too plain.

Hanka would show Charlotte in. After that, it was up to her to give the young woman an unforgettable Christmas at Bergfels Palace experience!

CHAPTER 15

Charlotte stopped in the driveway of Bergfels Palace and enjoyed the impressive sight. Snow was gently trickling down. With a frown, she remembered the weather forecast, which had predicted flurries for Christmas. *Hopefully not until the day after tomorrow, when I'm back home.*

She had agreed with the Count that she would go home first after the interview and photos. That way she could spend the time between the years with her parents and plan everything for the move to the palace. As long as she hadn't found a room in Bergfels, she could stay in a guest room. *Moving to the palace – oh, how that sounds!*

Slowly, she walked on, recalling her conversation with Melanie, with whom she had talked to for a solid hour in the already closed café after she had been promised the job. Her head had been full of questions that she had not dared to ask the Count. Moreover, she had wanted to make sure one more time that Ida was not actually staying at her father's estate. She would not survive a meeting.

Ida had made a joke of it and during their walk together had only pretended to be interested in Charlotte's professional future. She was sure of that. Of course, it was easy for Ida to make clever suggestions since she herself had no money worries as a Countess with a cushioned bank account.

The encounter with Melanie – well, with Ida, the real Countess – in the palace had thrown her completely off guard. Charlotte could only remember her stay back then in the archives in fragments. Completely agitated, she had sat in front of the chronicles of the Count's family and made notes, all of which were useless.

The next day, she had randomly incorporated the notes into her dissertation so as not to have to think about Melanie, alias Ida, all the time. Only to catch a rebuke from her adviser and reviewer a week later. All sources were mixed up and she had blithely confused the names of the Count's family with those of the royal family by marriage. Apart from that, as if by magic, Ida's name had crept in at random in its entirety.

What's more, Charlotte hadn't paid attention when updating, and some of the footnotes had simply disappeared. Fortunately, she had several backup copies, which she had used to reinsert the references, but it had still been an immense effort to straighten everything out and get everything in order. Bygones!

In the meantime, she had realized that the job offer wasn't so bad and had quickly given a written notice to her editor.

Today, she would conduct the interview with the Count and his son, and afterwards the archive would be open to her. She would hurry past the large picture hanging in front of the archive entrance, on which Ida was posing in a truly aristocratic manner, with her head bowed. And not have a queasy feeling about it. She had firmly resolved to do that!

As an employee, she was now permitted to make her notes, photograph documents, and rummage around in the holdings in complete peace of mind. Later, after her probationary period, she would be allowed to travel to Portugal to look through the family archives, as well as the other archives of the Count's in-laws in other European countries.

In her wildest dreams, history researchers were desperately scrambling for her doctoral thesis, which would, of course, be printed by a publishing house of repute!

She walked along the path that had been cleared of snow to the side entrance of the palace, which lay hidden behind the main wing. After her interview, Hanka had discreetly pointed out this entrance to her. She had knocked unknowingly on the large entrance gate, which had stood invitingly open to guests during her first visit to the palace, when Ida's game of hide-and-seek had been exposed.

In the meantime, I've become smarter, and soon I'll almost be part of the building's inventory. Not without pride, she smiled.

Just as she brought her hand to the bell, Hanka opened the door for her. Charlotte had a greeting on her lips, but the servant was quicker and welcomed her with a beaming smile.

"Ms. Weinhold, you're right on time, that's nice. Come on in! I'll show you your room before I take you to the interview."

Charlotte had difficulty following Hanka through the long corridors of the adjacent wing. After passing through quite a few doors, they came to the large reception hall that Charlotte knew from her previous visits. The guest room was as large as her entire apartment. She quickly unpacked her bag and sat down on the bed.

No pink four-poster bed, she noted, a little disappointed, *just an ordinary one.*

***

Half an hour later, there was a knock at her room door.

"Ms. Weinhold? You are expected now."

"Just a minute, I'm coming." She looked in the mirror and reached for her laptop bag, which also contained two voice recorders. For important interviews, she always set up two devices as a precaution – better safe than sorry.

"I'm taking you to the interview now," Hanka explained. Duh, that was why she was here, after all. "There will be tea and pastries. If you would like, you can have a little something for dinner after the interview."

A touch of nervousness came over Charlotte. This opportunity, which was offered to her today, was unique. This time she had matched Hanka's quick steps.

They approached the grand staircase. Charlotte peered cautiously over the laptop bag she held pressed against her. She didn't want to trip and fall down the steps.

"No, Ms. Weinhold, this way," she heard the servant's voice.

"Oh, I thought the Count's office was downstairs."

"Yes, but the interview will take place in a different, more comfortable room."

Charlotte scolded herself for being so hasty. How could she expect everything to happen in one and the same room? The palace had what felt like 150 rooms at its disposal. *It's just different from my little studio apartment.*

Hanka stopped in front of a squiggly wooden door. "Ready?" She smiled encouragingly at Charlotte.

"Hmm, ready!" Charlotte nodded affirmatively and stepped boldly through the door into a homey, Christmas-decorated room bathed in candlelight, and *White Christmas* played softly in the background and cracks of wood crackled in the fireplace.

"Wow," it escaped her. "Count of Bergfels-Blumenheide, excuse my frankness, but this is beautiful, really much more comfortable than in your office. I'm speechless!" And indeed, she was, for from a corner of the room stepped out not the Count, but Ida. Charlotte looked helplessly at the door, but it was closed, and Hanka had disappeared.

"Charlotte? My father and brother sent their apologies. They are both busy, as they always are before Christmas, organizing the Christmas hunt."

As always? Charlotte's mind raced. How could she have forgotten such a traditional date when it was regularly on the Count's official calendar? And why hadn't she remembered the shooting, which had been taking place for decades, when she was writing about it in her dissertation!

Headless, she ran to the heavy door. She braced herself against it, but the clunky part did not move a bit. She threw herself against the wood with all her might. Again, nothing happened.

"You had us locked up?" Horror spread through her. "I guess a Countess like you can get away with anything!" Charlotte snorted, crossing her arms in front of her chest, and leaning against the wooden door, out of breath.

"What impression must you have gotten from me? Of course, the door is open!"

Ida had rushed to her side and pushed down the door handle, which opened as if by magic. "But it opens inward." Charlotte would have liked to sink into the ground.

"By the way, if you want, I'll find you the blueprints, then you can get a picture of the building plan at your leisure," Ida suggested.

"I'd love to," Charlotte said, but she wasn't sure she wanted to take the job anymore. Melanie and the Count had assured her that Ida would not be at home and now this?

"As for us... I confess I set up our meeting this way because I really wanted to talk to you. I should have joined right after your confession that you were not the new cleaning lady for the café and revealed my true identity," Ida apologized. "I'm sure you're very hurt and hate me for it."

She had taken a few steps closer and pointed to a table setting.

"But please, sit down first! Would you like some tea?" The question was probably more rhetorical, because Ida had long since hurried to the table and poured her some of the steaming liquid.

If you think I'm here drinking your sinfully expensive tea and spilling on your hand-embroidered tablecloth with excitement, you're mistaken. I won't do you that favor. Even if something warm would do Charlotte good. She eyed the Countess, who wore a fine silk scarf around her shoulders. It actually stayed in place like glue, without slipping, as was always the case with Charlotte when she wore something like that.

"That's a surprise tactic," the words escaped. She gritted her teeth and reluctantly let herself sink into the chair. And here, *sinking into the chair* took on a whole new meaning – that's how comfortable and soft the upholstery fabric was. *So comfortable.*

No, she missed the simple wooden chairs in her little place that demanded an orthopedically correct, upright sitting position from her, even if they gave her the feeling of collapsing every time she leaned or moved when working on her thesis.

Meanwhile, she couldn't help herself and stroked her fingers over the velvet cover of the armrests.

"Is there something wrong with it?"

Charlotte winced. "No, everything is perfect. I'm sitting very comfortably."

"Do we want to talk first, or do you want to do the interview first? If I'm going to rush you like this,

I want you to decide on the course of our meeting. Go ahead!"

"The interview first." Assuming she could still get all the questions together.

"Well, let's do the interview first. We'll have to postpone the photos until tomorrow, when the whole family is gathered here."

"The whole family?"

"I assume that's not a problem for you? Or are you already expected at home by your parents tomorrow at noon?"

"No, it was agreed with the Count that I would stay here until tomorrow afternoon."

"Then fire away!"

Hectically, Charlotte rummaged for the dictation machines and pulled out her laptop. It took a while until everything was set up. With every second that she needed for these preparations, the panic increased.

It wasn't Melanie sitting here anymore, but Ida. How was she supposed to address her? She had never been so aware of the difference in status as she was at this moment.

She felt Ida's questioning looks resting on her. She cleared her throat.

"Countess Florde..."

"No way! Ida. Please call me Ida."

Hesitantly, Charlotte began with her list of questions. Ida answered as if shot out of a pistol. She truly knew every detail of her family's history. About the palace that their ancestors had inherited from former royal family and the palace that once belonged to them, as well as true and imaginary love stories about their inhabitants.

On and on, Ida told her stories, and neither noticed how much time had passed. Only when Hanka stood in the doorway and talked about the dinner that had been prepared did Charlotte feel how hungry she was. The cookies and tea had long since been consumed.

Charlotte had understood by now that Ida had no bad intentions with her little game. She was an educated person, full of wit and with many anecdotes about her family tree and relatives, without putting even one of them in a bad light. Given the turbulent family history she told her, it was certainly not easy to remain completely unbiased at all times. Charlotte became downright dizzy because not everything was written in the freely accessible works in the libraries.

The editors of the magazine *Interior Views from Noble Palaces* asked her for twenty-five double page spreads for the special issue, plus the photos of the Count's family. If the number of pages had seemed unattainable a few hours ago, she now realized that she had compiled material for several special issues and would probably have to keep it short.

"Charlotte, will you come with me next door to the dining room?" Ida snapped her out of her thoughts.

"After dinner, we'll talk more. Then you will also get a USB stick from me with the family tree and reproductions of important documents that we think need a closer look and processing. You can look at them at your leisure another day."

It was exactly the right thing for me to quit my job at the newspaper. I don't need an exaggerated interview. The special issue on Interior Views from Noble Palaces *will be a bestseller, my doctoral thesis will be a hit, and the scientists will really go for it after publication!*

ONE YEAR LATER

Ida's and Charlotte's packed suitcases waited in line outside the entrance. Charlotte's parents' trolley looked tiny next to it. Safely packed in another bag was the gilded statue Charlotte had won for her article on the Count's family and dedicated to her parents. It would have a prominent place in their living room.

Ida's whole family gathered to say goodbye to Charlotte, her parents, and Ida after spending Christmas together. Her parents went back home. Ida and Charlotte, on the other hand, traveled to Castelo Montanha, the palace of the Portuguese relatives, to visit the archives there and spend a short vacation in the region.

A vacation that truly came at the right time because Charlotte would then leave her work in the archives to take up a post-doctoral position at a renowned university not far from Bergfels.

Naturally, Ida had not had to do much persuading. The offer had been too tempting, and she was looking forward to the next step in her scientific career.

"Thank you very much for the invitation. We enjoyed the stay very much and haven't had such a nice Christmas for a long time," Charlotte's mother explained enthusiastically.

"It was a pleasure for us to have had you as guests," replied Ida's mother.

"You must definitely spend a few days with us in the summer at the cottage in the Alps," the Count added.

Charlotte gave Ida a warm smile. For sure they would all meet again in the summer. But not at the vacation home in the Alps... no, in Portugal. Because what they had not yet revealed was that they would use the time there not only for vacation and work in the archives, but also for planning their wedding festivities in the Castelo Montanha.

ACKNOWLEDGEMENT

Big thanks to my wife Petra, who gave the go-ahead for sending the story to my diligent first readers with a thumbs-up after first inspection.

Annika, Marita, Sandra and Uschi: I have taken many of your suggestions and critical comments into account in my revision and hope that the story has become more understandable and readable as a result!

And a big thank you goes to my German editor Senta Herrmann, who put the finishing touches on everything after a critical review.

I have made minor editorial changes and translated the story into English, and I am extremely grateful to Sierra Campbell, who tidied and polished the translation and weeded out false friends – without your help, I would be stuck and lost!

If you, dear reader, liked the story and find the time, I would appreciate a review on one of the many existing portals!

Contact: Claudine-Auteur@web.de

What's Christmas Without Walnut Cookies?

Theodora wanted to spend the lead-up to the holidays and Christmas Eve quietly at home. Alone. But everything turned out differently because her new tenant moved in with her teenage daughter at the end of November. And from then on, Theodora's highly appreciated walnuts suddenly disappear from the terrace. Who could be responsible for this?

The mother and teenager seem to celebrate the pre-Christmas season extensively. At that point, Theodora realized she must get rid of them as quickly as possible. But soon after, she became involved in their daily lives, more than she could ever have imagined.

Booklet, 48 pages
ISBN-10: 375684448X, ISBN-13: 978-3756844487
E-Book: ISBN-13: 9783756870721

A Date with Castle Ruins

Babsi is frustrated. The short vacation that was planned for her and her family in Bergfels Village is cancelled. The Christmas Market in Bergfels, which her wife wanted to report on, will not take place.

Furthermore, the bazaar, which her daughter, Hannah, was involved with planning this year, is in the balance. As if that wasn't annoying enough, Hannah and her friend also run into trouble with the law.

Their jaunt to the local ruins of Sturmstein Castle has unexpected consequences, in which a certain Countess Ida of Bergfels-Blumenheide is not uninvolved.

What none of them suspects: within the ruin's wrecked walls, the mouse, Murina, has to stand trial–only for doing people a favor, of all things.

In this short story about the ruins of Sturmstein Castle, the main characters of Claudia Haase's previously published short stories all join up, but the volume can also be read independently.

ISBN: 9783757887940. Release date: 24 Nov 2023

In German language:

Walnussplätzchen unterm Weihnachtsbaum (2020)

Athena und Murina. Eine vorweihnachtliche Geschichte rund um das Lesbenberatungstelefon im Kulturhaus für Frauen und Mädchen (2020)

Weihnachten im Schloss (2021)

Rendezvous mit einer Burgruine (2022)

Eine treue Gesellin mir zur Seite (Arbeitstitel, 2024)